Catch That Chicken!

Atinuke

illustrated by Angela Brooksbank

For Mara Menzies and Imani Sykes who first thought of a chicken chaser!
And for Lani-Grace, who is one! ~ A.

For my mother, known as Granny Chicken, because she loves chickens! ~ A.B.

WALKER BOOKS
AND SUBSIDIARIES
LONDON · BOSTON · SYDNEY · AUCKLAND

Notes: This story takes place in West Africa. Sannu means 'take it easy'

First published 2020 by Walker Books Ltd, 87 Vauxhall Walk, London SE11 5HJ ✪ Text © 2020 by Atinuke ✪ Illustrations © 2020 by Angela Brooksbank ✪ The right of Atinuke and Angela Brooksbank to be identified as the author and illustrator respectively of this work has been asserted by them in accordance with the Copyright Designs and Patents Act 1988 ✪ This book has been typeset in Shinn ✪ Printed in China ✪ All rights reserved ✪ No part of this book may be reproduced, transmitted or stored in an information retrieval system in any form or by any means, graphic, electronic or mechanical, including photocopying, taping and recording, without prior written permission from the publisher ✪ British Library Cataloguing in Publication Data: a catalogue record for this book is available from the British Library ✪ www.walker.co.uk
ISBN 978-1-4063-6361-6 ✪ 10 9 8 7 6 5 4 3 2 1

This is Lami.

Lami loves chickens.
Luckily Lami lives
in a compound ...

with lots and lots of chickens.

"Catch 'am, Lami! Catch 'am!"
shouts brother Bilal.

"Catch that chicken!"
shouts friend Fatima.

"Catch 'am, Lami! Catch 'am!"
shouts sister Sadia.

"Catch that chicken!"
shouts Nana Nadia.

"Catch that chicken!" shouts Daddy Danlami.

"Catch that chicken!" shouts Aunty Aisha.

Lami leans!

Lami lunges!

Lami leaps!

And Lami
catches her!

Lami is the **best** chicken catcher in the village.

Sister Sadia is speedy
at spelling.
But when it comes
to chickens ...

Lami
is speedier.

Friend Fatima is fast
at plaiting hair.

But when it comes
to chickens ...

Lami is faster.

Big brother Bilal
is brave with bulls.

But when it comes
to chickens ...

Lami is braver.

Until the day Lami chased that chicken through the pen.

"Sannu! Sannu!" shouted the uncles.

"Slow down!"

She chased that chicken round the compound.

"Sannu! Sannu!" shouted the aunties.

"SLOW DOWN!"

She chased that chicken up
the big baobab...

"Sannu! Sannu!"
shouted the elders.

"SLOW DOWN!"

But Lami scrambled speedily.

Lami snatched suddenly.

Lami slipped swiftly.

And
she fell!

She sprained her ankle

so badly it puffed up like the neck

of an angry lizard.

Lami cried.

It hurt and now she could not chase,

she could not climb,

and she could definitely not

catch chickens.

"If you are not careful

you will soon be best in the village

at crying," said Nana Nadia with a smile.

"It's not quick feet that catches chickens,

it's quick thinking."

Lami stared at her.

Lami thought.

She thought slowly ...

then she thought quicker

and quicker and ...

suddenly Lami knew

what to do!

She could make the chicken come to her!

"Catch that chicken!"
whispered Nana Nadia.

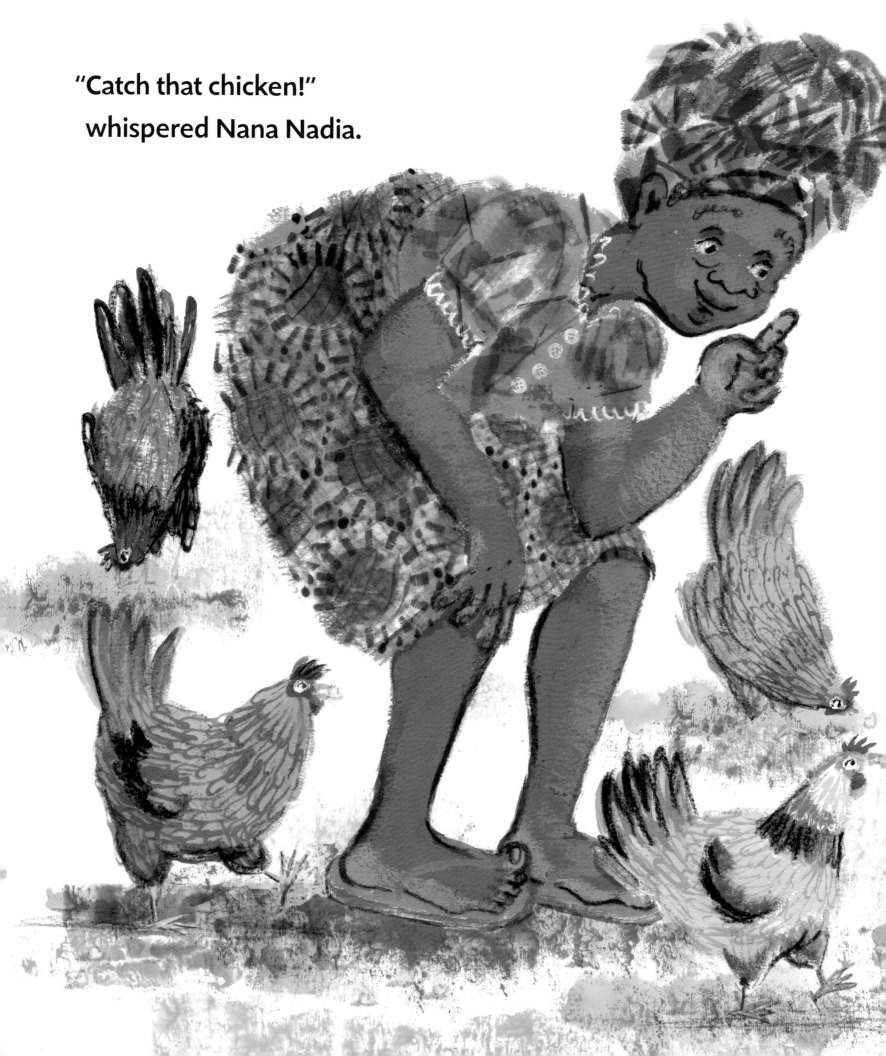

"Caught her!"
said Lami.

She is still the **best** chicken catcher in the village.

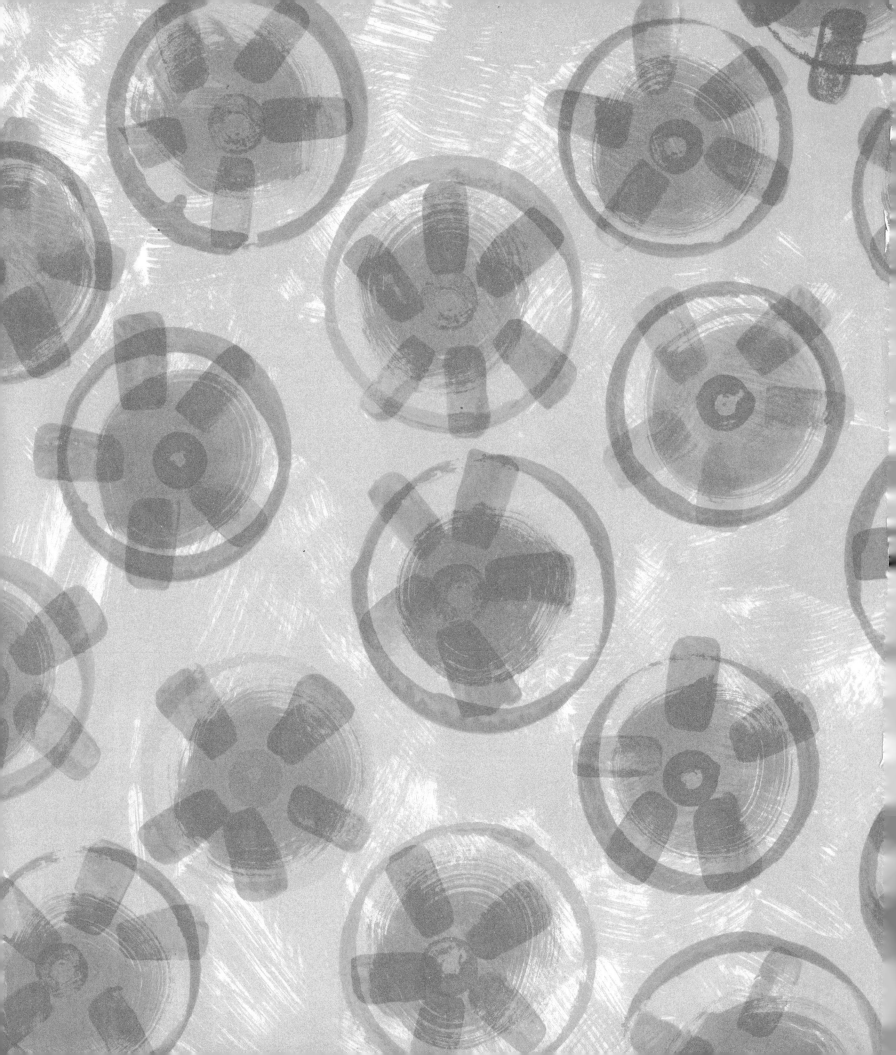